Billy and Fatcat were sailing the ocean blue,
which was something they liked to do now and then.

"We are noble seafaring explorers!" cried Billy.
"On the hunt for fun and adventure!"

THE JOLLY BADGER

Fatcat wondered when it would be time for a snack.

They swam and splashed,

and snoozed and sang,

and did a little spot of fishing.

They caught a boot, a very grumpy crab . . .

and a mysterious-looking bottle.
"A key," said Billy. "That's strange."

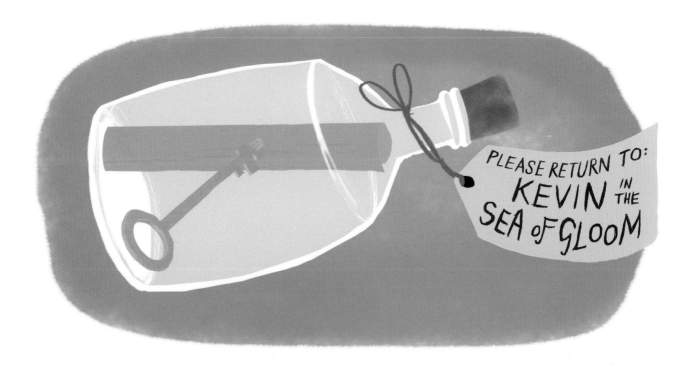

Billy uncorked the bottle and took out a map.

"Look, Fatcat! We're not that far away.
Why don't we find Kevin and give him back his key?"

First they would need
to navigate past
Skull Rock . . .

then sail through
shark-infested waters . . .

before entering the
SEA OF GLOOM.

"Let's go!" cried Billy.
And they set sail.

THE JOLLY BADGER

But then . . .

. . . a giant fishing net
flew down from the sky!

THE JOLLY BADGER

"Ahoy there, prisoners! My name is Captain Howl
and these are my fearsome shipmates, Quint and Brody.
And now *you're* in my pirate crew too!"

"But we're not pirates!" said Billy.
"We are noble seafaring explorers."

"Oh really?" said Captain Howl.
"Then why do you have a
TREASURE MAP?"

"We're returning this bottle to its rightful owner,"
said Billy. "So get your paws off, dog breath!"

But Captain Howl had other fiendish plans. "Piffle and nonsense – this must be the key to a treasure chest, and soon it will be mine, ALL MINE!"

"Crew!
Let us follow the map
and find these glorious riches!
Set sail at once!"

But as they approached Skull Rock the air was filled with swirling, whirling hypnotic music.

Captain Howl looked through his telescope and squealed in fright.

"I'm being lured!" he cried. "Lured to my doom
by these beautiful, musical mermaids!
We'll crash on to Skull Rock for sure!"

"Crew! Prepare to fire the cannons!
We have to stop that infernal singing!"

"Oh no!" gasped Billy.
She couldn't let him hurt
the mermaids.
She had to think fast.

"Wait! Captain, if you let us go,
I think I can help," she said.

"Really?" replied Captain Howl, who was shaking with fear.
"Crew, cut the prisoners free."

Billy searched through the pirates' loot
until she found what she was looking for.

"Here you go," she said to the mermaids.
"Make some noise!"

And they really did.

"Well, tickle my armpits – I'm being lured no more!"
said Captain Howl. "I could use a clever first mate like you."

Billy thought for a moment.

"Fine, I'll help you," she said, "but in return you must
set us free after we reach the Sea of Gloom. Deal?"

"It's a Pirate Promise!" hooted Captain Howl.

Once more the pirate ship set sail . . .

But soon the air was filled with a

SNAP SNAP SNAP!

Billy gasped as the boat was circled by deadly sharks.
They seemed hungry.

"We're done for," squealed Captain Howl.
"It's all over! Save me – I mean, save yourselves!"

"Don't worry, guys," said Billy. She rooted around in her hair.
"If there's one thing that sharks love to eat, it's . . .

VERY CHEWY TOFFEES!"

And then the sharks were too busy chomping on toffees to eat anyone. "Wow! Are you *sure* you're not a pirate?" asked Captain Howl.

"No way!" huffed Billy. "Pirates are smelly and mean."

"To be fair, Captain," said Brody, "we are a bit smelly."

And once more
the pirate ship set sail . . .

But then the sky grew dark and the sea became fierce.

"The kraken!" whispered Billy.

"We're going to need some bigger toffees . . ."

The kraken's great tentacles flailed and shook the ship into the air.

"None shall pass!" it bellowed. "And I mean NONE!
I've had it up to here with you lot sailing boats all over my sea!"

"Take them, not meeee!" cried Captain Howl, shoving Quint and Brody along the plank.

Billy had to think fast. She climbed up to the crow's nest.

she bellowed.

"Why, yes it is!" said the kraken.

"Then I think I have something that belongs to you," said Billy.

"Oh, how wonderful!" squealed Kevin. "You found my bottle! Oh thank you, noble seafarer, thank you!"

But Captain Howl wasn't so happy.
"Where are you going? Where's the treasure chest?" he hooted.

"Ooh no, there's no treasure chest," said Kevin.
"It's my front door key. I'm always losing it!
So I put spare ones in bottles and leave them all over the place.
Byeeee!"

howled Captain Howl, who was in a RAGE.

"That's it!" he said to Billy and Fatcat.
"You've ruined everything! We're meant to thieve
and steal, not help people. Now get off my boat –
you two are FISH FOOD!"

But then a giant fishing net flew down from the sky!

Quint and Brody had come to the rescue!

"We've had it with your fiendish ways, Howl," said Brody.
"Yeah, we don't want to be pirates no more," said Quint.

And Captain Howl was taken to a faraway desert island
to think long and hard about what he had done.

"Now let us head for adventure!" said Billy.
Fatcat gave a little cough.
"And snacks!" added Billy. "Adventure and snacks!"

And together they sailed onwards into the ocean blue.